Looking for Llamas

A SEEK-AND-FIND ADVENTURE

BuzzPop

BuzzPop

An imprint of Little Bee Books
251 Park Avenue South, New York, NY 10010
Copyright © 2018 by Egmont UK Limited
This BuzzPop edition, 2019
All rights reserved, including the right of reproduction in whole or in part in any form.
BuzzPop and associated colophon are trademarks of Little Bee Books.
Manufactured in China HUH 1019
First U.S. Edition
2 4 6 8 10 9 7 5 3
ISBN 978-1-4998-0986-2
buzzpopbooks.com

For more information about special discounts on bulk purchases,
please contact Little Bee Books at sales@littlebeebooks.com.

Contents

Introduction

The land where these llamas live may look like paradise, but this herd has itchy hooves! These curious llamas want to trot off to see the world and make some memories they'll never forget, playing hide-and-seek at each and every stop.

Look out for six llamas and their six cacti friends in each busy scene throughout the book. But be warned— they're pretty good at hiding. You'll find the answers at the back of the book, along with some extra items to spot.

Let's begin the grand llama world tour!

Meet the Herd!

No Probllama

Nothing is a problem for this laid-back llama. He's never in a rush to get anywhere, which sometimes makes traveling as part of a herd a problem! He often pops up in the strangest of hiding places.

Shama Llama Ding Dong

Perfectly preened at all times, Shama loves the limelight, but plays hide-and-seek to win! She laps up the applause if she's last to be found, although her fluffy pink leg warmers often give her away.

Llamanade

Llamanade is a homebody at heart and is a little nervous about his herd's globe-trotting adventures. He likes his own space, so is rarely found in the thick of things.

Drama Llama

Drama Llama is the head of the herd, or at least that's what she likes to tell herself. She's great at organizing everyone and keeps a detailed travel itinerary hidden under her fleece.

Charma Llama

Charma by name, charmer by nature! This smooth operator has impeccable manners, greeting everyone he meets with a kind word and a toothy grin. Charma loves traveling to exotic places in search of adventure.

Kendrick Llama

Kendrick is the coolest kid in the flock! He's young, with bags of energy and a certain star quality. He'll happily pose for a selfie with anyone who asks.

Say Hi to the Cacti!

Cal and Caz

A pair of prickly pears! Twins Cal and Caz constantly squabble, but don't like to stray too far from one another.

Camilla

A kindly cactus, Camilla is often the first to be found in games of hide-and-seek due to her gleeful giggle.

Carlo

Carlo is mad about music and sways in time to the beat whenever the band starts up. Tunes played on a pan flute are his absolute favorite!

Casper

Casper loves to tell anyone who'll listen that he's 167 years young. When he's not fast asleep, he's scouting out the best place for his next nap.

Carrie

All-seeing, nothing passes Carrie by—she towers over the other cacti. Truth be told, she's a bit of a gossip.

Bon Voyage!

The llamas have made it down from the mountains and their cacti buddies have hitched a ride, too! Now they just have to clear airport security before jetting off on their first adventure!

Kendrick's excitement levels are off the chart, while Llamanade would be glad if he could head straight back home and hit the hay.

Spot all six traveling llamas and six cacti if you can!

Llamas in the Bahamas

The llamas have arrived at their destination—the tropical islands of the Bahamas! Here's where they kick back, relax, and soak up some sun. Bliss!

Shama Llama is having a splashing time while No Probllama is hanging out with an ice cream cone.

Look out for six beach llamas and their six cacti friends.

Skate Park Search

The llamas may be skating newbies, but that won't stop them from attempting some insane moves at the local skate park. Llamanade would love to try some scooter stunts—if only he were a little braver! The guys on BMXs are blowing No Probllama's mind.

Locate the six skating llamas and their six cacti buddies.

Movie Night

Lights, Llamas, Action! Our llamas have trotted into town to catch the latest blockbuster movie: *The Alpacalypse 2*. The sweet scent of popcorn was too good to resist for Shama while Kendrick's snack of choice is a giant hot dog.

Find six moviegoing llamas and their six spiky friends.

Pet Show

Now our herd has hoofed it down to a pet show—if only they had entered! There are cute and cuddly pets, weird and wonderful pets, and pets that look like their owners. The llamas go wild for the animal acts in the show! Shama has decided she wants a pet poodle, while a goldfish is more Llamanade's speed.

Find all six llamas and six cacti among the pets.

Winter Wonderland

Brrr! It's chilly out on the mountain, where skiers, snowboarders, tobogganists, and llamas are all sharing the slopes. Luckily, our woolly wanderers are never without their coats! Kendrick's too cool for ski school and No Probllama has never felt more chilled!

Spot six wintry llamas and find six cacti, too.

A Passion for Fashion

Our *dah-lling* llamas have headed to Paris for Fashion Week. Their fur has been styled, their outfits chosen, and now they're ready to strike a pose! No Probllama loves his new look and is happily strutting his stuff on the catwalk!

Find six llamas and six cool cacti in the scene.

21

Soccer Spirit

It's at fever pitch at the soccer stadium as the herd head over to see their very first match. Barcellama are taking on Woolly Wanderers in the Chompions League and the teams are ready to go. Wait, what's this? Some llamas are on the field! They think it's all edible . . . it is now! *Munch!*

Spot a team of llamas and a team of cacti. There are six per side!

Las Vegas Wedding

Love is in the air in sunny Las Vegas as another happy couple ties the knot. Llamanade is hoping to see the bride and groom get hitched without a hitch while *g-llama-rous* Shama Llama is a favorite to catch the bride's bouquet.

Locate six lovely llamas and their six cacti friends.

City Carnival

Llamas love to party and the city carnival is the perfect place! There are some truly tremendous sights on display and the herd has met some colorful characters. Join Kendrick, Charma, and co as they move their hooves and get into the groove!

Can you spot six partying llamas and six cacti?

Shopping Trip

If there's one thing llamas love to do, it's shop!
No Probllama is checking out some new pajamas while
Llamanade thinks all the stores are out to fleece him!
He's a glass-*hoof*-empty kinda llama.

**Spot six llamas shopping 'til
they drop and six cacti.**

Llamafest

Our lucky llamas have bagged themselves a ticket each for the hottest festival in town— Llamafest! Drama Llama has dug out her rain boots while Kendrick Llama takes center stage.

Look for six dancing llamas and their six prickly cacti friends.

Dance Floor Divas

While the llamas' world tour has been *baa-rilliant*, the herd is beginning to miss the peace and quiet of mountain life. The flights home are booked, but the llamas can't bow out without one last party. Llama mia, here we go again!

Look for six dancing llamas and their six cacti friends.

Answers

Bon Voyage!

Lots more to spot!

A girl reading

Two people fighting over one suitcase

An inflatable flamingo

A handshake

Two dancing girls

A man filming

A lost balloon

A pair of skis

A janitor

Lots more to spot!

A giant crab

A seagull thief

A metal detector

A sandy ice cream

A scuba diver

A large drinks order

A big sandcastle

An angry lifeguard

A posing muscleman

A banana boat

Llamas in the Bahamas

Skate Park Search

Lots more to spot!

- A flat tire
- An enormous pigeon
- A bearded man wearing sunglasses
- A face on a wall
- A backward boarder
- A spilled drink
- An awesome granny
- A pigeon dance-off
- A skating dog

Lots more to spot!

- An unusually tall man
- A pair of winged 3-D glasses
- An autographing actor
- A banana peel
- A latecomer
- An oversized statuette
- An exit sign
- A movie magazine
- An alien audience member
- A backward baseball cap

Movie Night

Pet Show

Lots more to spot!

- An ostrich rider
- A dog that looks like its owner
- A sunflower with a face
- A cowboy pup
- A skateboarding tortoise
- An acrobatic parrot
- A prizewinning goldfish
- A solitary stick insect
- The pinkest of poodles
- An unfortunate puddle

Lots more to spot!

- A human snowball
- A snowboarding dog
- A mad moose
- An abominable snowman
- A helmet with antlers
- A snowman in progress
- Eight helpful huskies
- A sleeping snow angel
- A flying bobsled

Winter Wonderland

A Passion for Fashion

Lots more to spot!

A sneaky snack

A forgotten hairbrush

A pair of pigeons

A faux fur coat

A backward baseball cap

A random robot

A green kilt

A purple cactus

An apple core

A white puppy

Lots more to spot!

An inflatable trophy

A flying shoe

A drone

A mischievous mole

A horned helmet

A random rugby ball

A conductor

A field-invading dog

A mega mascot

A team floss

Soccer Spirit

Las Vegas Wedding

Lots more to spot!

A falling coconut

A pair of high heels

A magical mermaid

Some happy hot-tubbers

An Elvis all in black

A dog in a purse

A packed roller coaster

A toppling cake topper

Lots more to spot!

An octopus costume

A pair of binoculars

A big lollipop

A manhole escapee

A playful pup

Bunny ears

A Hula-Hoop

Some helpful garbage-pickers

A colorful fan

City Carnival

Shopping Trip

Lots more to spot!

A toddler tantrum

A swirly lollipop

A pooch in a handbag

A pink balloon

A kid on crutches

A number 7 shirt

A boy in a bush

A pile of gifts

Llamafest

Lots more to spot!

A jolly juggler

A cozy campfire

A pair of Porta Potties

A barbecue line

A tambourine dance

A big dog

An acoustic guitar

A treasure chest

Lots more to spot!

Some soda on ice

Two pesky paparazzi

Two friends flossing

A woman in a spotted dress

A pair of pink fairy wings

A silver disco ball

The word "disco"

A pink-haired DJ

A wheelchair raver

Dance Floor Divas